A sad princess sat at her castle window.
She had never laughed, and didn't know
how to. Her mum and dad hoped that one
day, somebody would make their daughter
smile.

To Zoë, Katy and Philippa

LAZY JACK

Tony Ross

PUFFIN BOOKS

Once, a boy called Jack lived with his mother.
Jack was probably the laziest person in the whole world,
and he would just sit around while his mother did all the
work.

At last, Jack's mother could stand no more of his
laziness.

"Unless you get out and get a job," she shouted,
"you'll get no more meals from me! You'll have to wash
your own socks too."

"Okay," said Jack, and he went to work for a farmer,
who paid him a shiny pound.

On the way home, Jack had to jump over a stream, and he dropped the pound into the water.

Of course, his mother was angry,

"Twit!" she cried. "You should have put it in your jacket pocket."

"Okay," said Jack. "I'll do so next time."

Next day, Jack went to work for a cow keeper, who gave him a jug of milk for his wages.

Remembering his mother's advice, he poured the milk into his pocket, and went home.

"Silly sausage head!" shouted his mother. "You should have carried the jug on your head."

"Okay," said Jack. "I'll do so next time."

Next, Jack went to work at the dairy. For payment, he was given a fine cheese, all for himself.

Remembering his mother's advice, he put the cheese on his head. When he got it home, it had melted into a gooey mess.

"Gormless beetle brain!" screeched his mother. "You should have carried it in your arms."

"Okay," said Jack. "I'll do so next time."

Jack's next job was in a sausage factory, where he was given a cat as payment.

Remembering his mother's advice, he carried the cat home in his arms.

The cat was a nasty beast who hated being picked up.

When Jack got home, he was scratched to bits.
  "Jelly-headed hen brain!" yelled his mother. "You should have pulled it behind you on a string."
  "Okay," said Jack. "I'll do so next time."
  Next day, he went to work in a bakery.

The bakers were pleased with Jack's work, and they gave him a cake for his trouble.

Remembering his mother's advice, Jack pulled it home behind him on a string.

"Nitwitted pinhead!" shouted his mother. "You should have carried it on your back."

"Okay," said Jack, "I'll do so next time."

Next, Jack went to work in a stable.

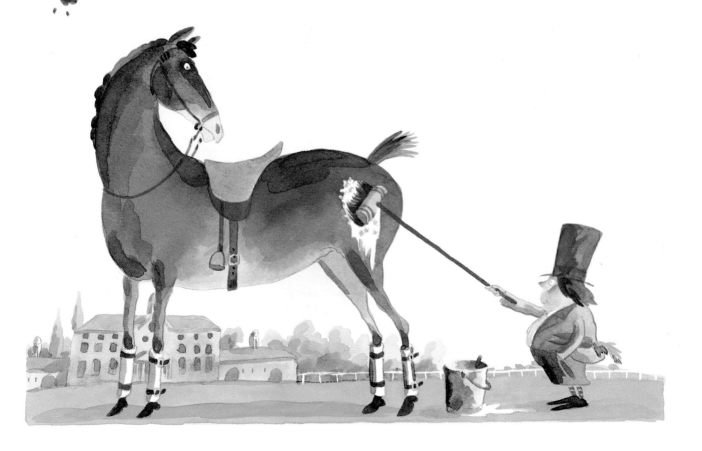

When the work was finished, the owner of the stable gave Jack a donkey as payment.

Remembering his mother's advice, Jack heaved the donkey onto his shoulders.

It was not easy, not easy at all, and Jack staggered away towards his home.

His way took him past the castle of the sad princess who could not smile, and she happened to be sitting at her window.

　　She watched Jack stagger by, with his donkey on his back...

　　　　He looked so funny...

that the sad princess burst out laughing.

The princess's mum and dad were so happy, they let Jack marry her.

The princess was happy to have such a funny husband . . . and Jack was happy, because he never had to work again.